Dear Parent:
Your child's love of reading starts here!

Every child learns to read in a different way and at his or her own speed. Some go back and forth between reading levels and read favorite books again and again. Others read through each level in order. You can help your young reader improve and become more confident by encouraging his or her own interests and abilities. From books your child reads with you to the first books he or she reads alone, there are I Can Read Books for every stage of reading:

SHARED READING
Basic language, word repetition, and whimsical illustrations, ideal for sharing with your emergent reader

BEGINNING READING
Short sentences, familiar words, and simple concepts for children eager to read on their own

READING WITH HELP
Engaging stories, longer sentences, and language play for developing readers

READING ALONE
Complex plots, challenging vocabulary, and high-interest topics for the independent reader

ADVANCED READING
Short paragraphs, chapters, and exciting themes for the perfect bridge to chapter books

I Can Read Books have introduced children to the joy of reading since 1957. Featuring award-winning authors and illustrators and a fabulous cast of beloved characters, I Can Read Books set the standard for beginning readers.

A lifetime of discovery begins with the magical words "I Can Read!"

Visit www.icanread.com for information
on enriching your child's reading experience.

For information address HarperCollins Children's Books, a division of HarperCollins Publishers, 10 East 53rd Street, New York, NY 10022.
www.icanread.com

Library of Congress catalog card number: 2008937118
ISBN 978-0-06-162619-7
Typography by Joe Merkel

11 12 13 LP/WOR 10 9 8 7 6 5 ❖ First Edition

ead!
READING
2
WITH HELP

THE AMAZING SPIDER-MAN

Spider-Man Versus Kraven

by Susan Hill
pictures by Andie Tong
colors by Jeremy Roberts

HarperCollins*Publishers*

PETER PARKER

Peter Parker is a very
good student.

MR. JAMESON

Peter works for Mr. Jameson
at the *Daily Bugle*.

KRAVEN THE HUNTER

Kraven the Hunter is one evil guy
He collects endangered animals,
but not to save them.
He just wants them for himself.

SPIDER-MAN

Peter has a secret identity.
He is Spider-Man!

"Grab your camera, Parker!"
yelled Mr. Jameson.

"What's up?" Peter Parker asked

his boss at the *Daily Bugle*.

"Another rare animal was stolen

from the zoo!" Mr. Jameson said.

Peter hurried to the zoo.

He saw a strange man

wearing animal skins!

The man unlocked a tiger's cage.

Peter quickly stuck his camera

to the wall with webbing.

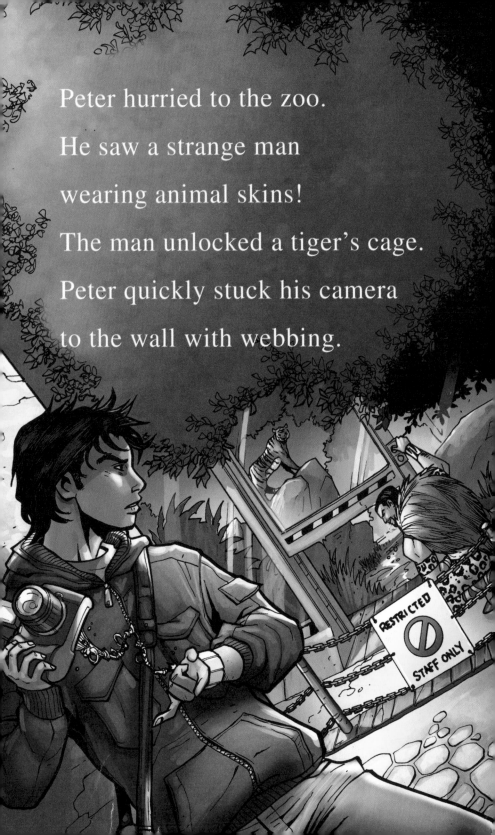

RESTRICTED

STAFF ONLY

Peter changed into his costume.

Peter does not just take pictures.

He also fights crime.

Peter Parker is Spider-Man!

He swung to the cage and locked it.

The tiger was safe!

Then Spidey swung around
and quickly shot a web
to trap the bad guy.

"Who are you?" said Spidey.
"And may I give you a ride
to the police station?"

The man laughed.

Then he broke through

Spider-Man's web!

"I'm Kraven the Hunter!"

he yelled.

Spider-Man jumped out of the way as Kraven attacked.

"I am a great hunter," Kraven said. "I have caught hundreds of animals for my collection!"

"But I had nothing left to hunt, until I saw you!" Kraven yelled.

"Me?" said Spider-Man.

Kraven grabbed Spider-Man
and held him in a powerful grip.

Quickly, Spider-Man broke free.

He hit Kraven hard.

"Take that, Leopard Pants!"

said Spider-Man.

Kraven leaped out of the way.
"A good hunter always has
a few tricks up his sleeves,"
he said.

Spider-Man jumped on Kraven's back.

"You don't have any sleeves!"

said Spidey.

"I've got you now!"

"No, you don't!" Kraven yelled.

Kraven took out something

small and sharp.

Spider-Man didn't see it.

His spider-sense gave him a warning.

But what was wrong?

As Spider-Man fought,

Kraven scratched him!

Spider-Man fell from Kraven's back.

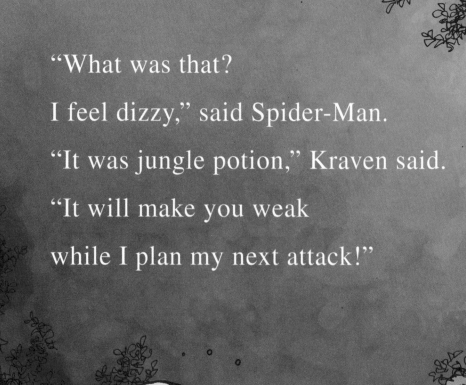

"What was that?

I feel dizzy," said Spider-Man.

"It was jungle potion," Kraven said.

"It will make you weak

while I plan my next attack!"

"Remember the law of the jungle,"

Kraven said.

"Hunt or be hunted!"

Then he ran away into the night.

The potion kept Spider-Man weak.

His hands shook

and his head hurt.

"I can't fight crime like this,"
Spider-Man said.
"If Kraven finds me,
he'll trap me for his collection."

Then Spider-Man remembered
what Kraven had said.
Hunt or be hunted.
Spidey knew what he had to do.

Spider-Man looked for Kraven

all night long.

At last, his spider-sense

led him to the hunter's hideout.

Spider-Man saw the stolen animals
and one empty cage.

"That cage will not be for me!"

Spider-Man said to himself.

"Too many people need me!"

Suddenly, Spider-Man felt strong!

Spider-Man jumped into the room.

Kraven leaped to his feet.

"It was a mistake for you to come.

Now I will trap you!" Kraven said.

"Just try!" said Spidey.

Spider-Man shot a web

to catch Kraven.

Kraven broke the web and attacked!

But Spider-Man shot another web!

And another!

And another!

This time, the webs held.

Spider-Man felt much better.

He had stopped Kraven

and found the missing animals.

Spider-Man put Kraven in the cage.

He made sure to take some pictures

for the newspaper.

"I'll get you yet!" said Kraven.

"But I must know one thing.

Are you man or beast?"

Peter smiled behind his mask.

"I'm Spider-Man!" he said.